I0572656

HE DID
IT AGAIN

HE DID IT AGAIN

IT AGAIN

A Gay Love Story

by

David Olin Tullis

Published by
Tullisian Books
Little Rock Arkansas
TullisianBooks@davidolintullis.com

This is a work of fiction.

ISBN: 978-0-9988855-3-7
(Softcover)

Date of First Publication:
January 15, 2002

Date of Re-release:
April 25, 2025

Table of Contents

Chapter One - Christmas

Chapter Two - New Year's Eve

Chapter Three - The Invitations

Chapter Four - The Wedding

Chapter Five – Conclusion

Chapter One
Christmas

"If you ever do this again, don't expect me to be there."

It had been seventeen years since Luke heard those shocking words. It is surprising just how often he is reminded of that sentence, but it is not surprising that it came to mind on that Christmas night a few years ago.

Luke and a group of his friends (his chosen family), all single, agreed several years ago to celebrate Thanksgiving together. Luke agreed to host, and everyone agreed to share in the preparation of dinner. Everyone had such a wonderful time that it has become an annual tradition. Those who have the space share the hosting duties and everyone contributes to the meal.

Christmas, though, is different for Luke. Some members of the group also get together for Christmas, but for Luke, Christmas is all about (real) family. He was especially looking forward to this Christmas because every family member was going to be together. This had not happened for several years. Sharing Christmas dinner and the gift exchange would be his parents (their house), his paternal grandparents, his brother and sister-in-law, his sister and brother-in-law, and his four nieces and nephews.

As always, he would drive down on the twenty-third, his mother's birthday, and return home on the twenty-sixth. It is about a six-and-a-half-hour drive, and he wanted to be at his parents' house by four in the afternoon. He had one extra stop along the way (more about that later), but it should not really add much time to his drive.

Luke carefully gathered everything that he needed to take with him. He spoke aloud as he named off everything. Luggage (the contents of which were called out previously in the bedroom), Christmas gifts (elegantly wrapped in this year's color scheme – glossy white paper with multi-colored grosgrain ribbon), his "good" camera, and his homemade chocolate walnut fudge and peanut brittle (requested by his mother because she says he makes the best fudge and peanut brittle).

Luke was quite happy when he first went outside and saw that it was a cloudy day. He much preferred to drive on cloudy days rather than worry about the sun in his eyes.

The car was packed, and one more trip inside the house to grab a cola and lock the doors was all he had left to do. At nine seventeen, he pulled out of the driveway. He was right on schedule.

Luke really did not mind this drive, even if it was more than six hours. For all but the last forty minutes or so, it was interstate highway driving. Traffic never seemed that heavy, even on holidays, and it had mostly wooded and pastoral views. Overall, a calm and pleasant drive.

At about the halfway point, Luke made his first stop. There was a rest area that was always a notch or two above most other rest areas. The landscaping was incredibly beautiful, and the restrooms were spotlessly clean.

As he made a right turn into the parking lot, he noticed that there were three big trucks parked in their designated spots, but only one car in the regular parking spots. It seemed a bit odd with all the holiday travelers on the road.

Another thing that he immediately noticed were Christmas lights, which he had never seen before. The building was outlined in multi-colored lights, but the focal point was a Christmas tree. It was a large White Spruce that was always there, but now it was completely covered in multi-colored lights and there was a large gold star on the top. It reminded Luke of a smaller version of the famous Rockefeller Center Christmas Tree in New York. It was absolutely spectacular. He walked toward the tree to get a close-up look and he noticed a small red and gold sign that read "Holiday lights courtesy of The Brooks Family Foundation." He had no idea who the Brooks family was, but he said a thank you, aloud, to them.

He decided to walk back to his car and get his camera. He needed to get pictures of this in case it never happened again.

Thinking it would look odd if he took a camera into the men's room, he walked back to his car after getting some good pictures of the Christmas lights.

He walked into the deserted men's room. The smell of bleach and lemon filled the air. Whomever is responsible for cleaning the place should get a raise. They are doing an exemplary job.

Since no one else was in there, he just walked up to the nearest urinal. He then simply crossed the room to the first sink to wash his hands. Before he even turned on the water, the door opened. It is our nature to be curious, so without even thinking about it, he turned his head to see who was coming into the room. Just that small act triggered a very unpleasant memory. When Luke was a fifth-grade student, one teacher, Ms. Connie, taught all his classes – except for math. For reasons he never knew, Ms. Browne darkened the classroom every afternoon to teach math. The doorway was in the back of the room. As it is human nature to be curious, every day when Ms. Browne walked into the room, at least a few of the students would always turn to see who was coming in. This infuriated Ms. Browne, and she did not hesitate to let them know about it – almost daily. It was her opinion that everyone should know it was time for her to come in, so there should be no reason to turn around and look. To most people it would not be important, but it sure did get on her last nerve. Ms. Browne remains the single most unpleasant person Luke has ever known.

Of course, that memory lasted only a second or two before Luke's thoughts went to the gentleman who just walked in. He did not stare. His eyes did not linger. But he did notice a very handsome man, just a little older than Luke. Most notable were his expensive looking clothes. He was beautifully dressed. A quick thought went through Luke's mind that most men would feel very dressed up in those clothes, but to this man they were probably just his casual traveling clothes.

After the brief glance, Luke turned around and began washing his hands. There was a mirror above the sink and Luke noticed that this man's body was still turned toward the urinal, but he had turned his head and was looking directly at Luke. He did have a lovely smile. He did not say anything. He just continued to stare at Luke.

Luke finished washing his hands and had to walk a step or two away from the mirror to use the hand dryer. He glanced up from the hand dryer. The stranger was still looking at him.

Having never done anything like this in his life, on his way to the door, Luke walked up to the stranger, placed his hands on his shoulders, and gently kissed him on the cheek.

"Merry Christmas," Luke told the man and walked toward the door.

"Wait. Please wait for me," the man said to Luke as the door was closing. He had no idea if Luke had even heard him.

Luke had, in fact, heard the man and waited in the breezeway that separated the two restrooms. Standing there, Luke became aware that the wind had picked up and it felt as if the temperature had dropped a little.

The well-dressed stranger came out of the restroom and gave a relieved smile when he saw Luke standing there.

"I've never done anything like that before. Please believe me. And thank you for being a gentleman. You could have gotten upset," he said.

"It's fine. I am certainly not upset. In fact, I am a little flattered. But be careful. It's not always safe," Luke replied.

"You seem genuinely nice. I would love to stay connected if you are willing. But's it's fine if you don't want to," the man said as he reached into his pocket and pulled out a leather card case. He offered one of the cards to Luke.

Luke accepted the card and reached into his own back pocket and pulled out his wallet. He placed the card in the wallet and returned it to his pocket. Oddly, though, he never actually looked at the card.

The stranger had noticed that Luke did not look at the card. He took that to mean that Luke was not interested in any further communication.

"You've probably got a long drive ahead of you. I know I do. Have a safe trip and a wonderful holiday," he said to Luke.

"You, too," Luke said as they both started walking toward their cars.

As Luke reached his car, the stranger looked toward him and yelled, "Happy New Year."

The stranger was in his car before Luke could reply.

Luke sat in his car for a few moments thinking about what had just happened. He began to question his own behavior. Perhaps he had not handled that situation correctly. He had not done anything wrong - really - and he finally convinced himself of that.

Luke was still on schedule to reach his parents' house by four o'clock. He turned the radio on to a station that was playing only Christmas music and drove peacefully down the highway singing along.

He had not gone that far from the rest area when he noticed a few – very few actually – snowflakes swirling in the air in front of him. He had checked the forecast before he left home and the possibility of snow was not even mentioned, so he was not worried that it would cause a driving problem for him.

After driving another hour or so, Luke knew that the extra stop that he wanted to make on this trip would be coming up soon, but he just did not know exactly where it was. He remembered that it was approximately five hours into the trip, which meant it was about ninety minutes from his destination. He knew he would have to really pay attention and watch for it. If he missed it, he would not get another chance until next Christmas.

The snow still seemed light as it was falling, but it was beginning to accumulate on the grass.

Staying in the right lane, Luke slowed down a little bit to make it easier to see all around him. He had to stay focused on the road, of course, but he needed to be very aware of what was on the right side of the road.

There it was, visible only in the winter when the trees are bare. He looked at the clock in the car.

He had been on the road exactly five hours. It was just where he remembered it to be.

Down an embankment and beyond a thick row of trees, on the edge of an enormous pasture, was a single grave enclosed in an ornate, black, wrought iron fence. On the side of the fence closest to the highway hung a simple green wreath with a large red bow.

To Luke, there was something so beautifully serene about this sight. He had seen this grave almost every December on his way to spend Christmas with his family. A few times he was not paying attention and drove past it. He had never stopped to see it up close or to take a picture, but this year he was.

The plan was to walk down to the grave to get a close-up view and to read the name and dates on the monument. And, of course, to take pictures. That is why he brought the camera. Well, part of that plan was not happening this year. The embankment was much deeper and much steeper than he had remembered. Add in the thin layer of snow on it and it would be extremely easy to get down there, but impossible to get back up to his car. Well, there is always next year.

Luke still planned to take good photographs. He was hoping, with the zoom lens, that he might be able to read anything that was carved on this side of the monument.

Looking directly down at the grave, symmetrically, gave him the best shot. However, the Christmas wreath blocked the view of the monument. A side angle, though, gave him an unobstructed view of the single monument. Luke assumed that the single monument meant that there was only one person buried down there.

Luke got the best shots possible, given the circumstances, and began walking back to his car. He continued to look at the gravesite as he walked. Suddenly, the most amazing thing happened. A small hole opened in the clouds and a narrow beam of sunlight shone directly down on the gravesite – just the gravesite. Luke did not waste a second and took a picture of this remarkable sight. Just as he snapped the picture, the clouds moved, and the beam of light disappeared. Luke had no idea for a moment if he was able to capture the light or not.

He hesitated just a moment, not wanting to be disappointed, before looking at the digital LCD display screen on his camera. He felt relieved. The image was perfect. He kept staring at the screen, in amazement. He was so moved by the beauty of it that tears fell down his cheeks.

Luke knew that if the rest of his trip were this good, it would be a perfect Christmas.

The next ninety miles seemed to go by in the blink of an eye. Luke pulled into his parents' driveway at five minutes until four. He had stayed right on schedule. Even after sitting in the car for hours, he felt exhilarated.

Luke's parents live on a quiet cul-de-sac. There are twelve houses on this street. Several years ago, the twelve homeowners decided to decorate their houses based on The Twelve Days of Christmas. Based on the order of the houses, his parents' theme was "eleven Lords a leaping." Luke was happy to see that the tradition continued. He secretly thought that it is funny that his parents have the gayest looking house in the neighborhood.

The light snowfall that Luke encountered along the way had not made its way to his hometown. He was hoping that it would by morning.

Although Christmas was the number one reason for this trip, Luke's mother's birthday was a close second. When she was growing up, her birthdays were barely acknowledged. Her family was so focused on Christmas that they practically ignored her birthday. That is certainly no longer the case.

Many years ago, quite by accident, a new tradition was born. It started out simple enough. Luke's immediate family offered to take her out to her favorite restaurant for a birthday dinner. Even then, she would not accept gifts, but a dinner out was happily accepted. Luke's father even called the restaurant to arrange for them to serve a birthday cake decorated with her favorite flower, tulips.

Their best friends – and next-door neighbors – heard about the birthday dinner and decided to surprise her and show up at the restaurant to help celebrate her birthday.

Her birthday has been celebrated the same way every year since. The only difference now is the number of participants. They now require an entire private dining room to accommodate all the friends and family that show up to celebrate her birthday. The birthday cake is still decorated with tulips every year, but the size of the cake has grown much larger.

Day one of Luke's four-day trip had come to a perfect conclusion.

Day two, Christmas Eve, it seemed, was going to be a very stress-free, laid back, kind of day. Everyone slept a little later than usual. That was nice. The rest of the day was just going to be last-minute gift wrapping, some light house cleaning, and getting a head-start on Christmas dinner.

Luke had asked his mother if there were any last-minute items she needed from the supermarket. She said no, so he was surprised that afternoon when she asked him to drive her to the mall.

"The mall? On Christmas Eve? Do you really want – or need – to deal with the crowd of people who will probably be there?" he asked.

"One store. In and out. It won't be a big deal," she tried to assure him.

"OK, let us go now. You know all the stores will close early today," Luke replied.

The parking lot was just as full as Luke expected it to be, but he lucked into a good parking spot by the entrance that his mother wanted to use. She jumped out of the car and hurried toward the entrance as if she were on a television game show and was trying to beat the clock. Luke followed right behind her.

She had not even told him what she wanted to buy and, it being Christmas, he did not want to ask any questions. She made a beeline for the most elegant store in town, Fontaine Fine Jewelry. It is not the kind of store that always has a crowd. Many people would be too intimidated to even go in, but that would not stop them from doing some serious window shopping.

Luke's mother knew precisely what she wanted, a diamond cross necklace that was in the window. The salesman was quite familiar with it and reached into a drawer below a display case and pulled out one of their distinctive navy and gold boxes. With a subtle flair, he opened the box to reveal an extremely beautiful gold and diamond cross that really sparkled beneath the overhead lights.

"Perfect. I'll take it," she told the salesman, much to his delight.

The salesman escorted Luke and his mother to a desk at the back of the store. All three sat down and, as he began to write up the sale, Luke's mother searched her purse for her card.

"Honey, I must have left my debit card in my other purse. Will you just give him yours?" she asked of Luke.

That immediately gave Luke an odd feeling, but not wanting to embarrass anyone, he reached into his wallet and laid his debit card on the desk in front of the salesman.

He returned the card to Luke and handed his mother a glossy navy and gold shopping bag which held the necklace. They all politely wished each other a Merry Christmas and Luke and his mother were ready to return home.

Nothing more was said that evening about the diamond necklace.

Christmas Eve, day two of his trip, had been a good day, just not perfect.

He did not know if it was his parents' subtle way to getting him out of bed, but Luke was awakened by the lovely sound of Christmas carols coming from the family room. He went straight from his bed to the window to see if it had snowed last night. Indeed, it had. Like he had seen on the drive down, a light snow had fallen, just enough to almost cover the grass, but certainly enough to call it a white Christmas.

The rest of the family was not due to arrive until after eleven, so Luke went out in his pajamas to greet his parents. He would make himself "presentable" before anyone else got there.

Stepping into the family room, Luke was overcome with a feeling of utter contentment. The Christmas tree lights, along with the gently cracking fire in the fireplace, gave the entire room a wonderful glow. The carols that woke him up were still playing and his mother's early start to Christmas dinner already filled the house with delicious smells.

By eleven thirty, the entire family had arrived and filled the house with talking and laughter. The four grandchildren had to tell everyone what Santa Claus had brought them. In almost no time at all, they had looked at every present under the tree to see which ones were theirs. They were good, though. They did not try to unwrap any of them. They knew that they had to wait until after lunch.

Around noon, the doorbell rang. Luke thought it was very odd. Everyone that he expected to be there had already arrived. He just happened to be the closest one to the front door, so he started walking that direction.

"I'll get it. I'll get it," his mother yelled from the kitchen.

Luke was almost to the front door, but he stopped and waited for his mother to open the door.

A young woman, quite pretty and around Luke's age, stood there holding two white boxes.

"Come on in. I'm so glad that you could make it," his mother told her.

She stepped into the foyer.

"Luke, dear, take her coat and hang it up, please."

The woman handed the white boxes to his mother as Luke helped with her coat.

Holding the boxes up slightly, Luke's mother asked what was in them.

"The pies I promised. One is chocolate cream and the other is pecan," she replied.

"Two of our favorites. Thank you so much. Why don't you come to the kitchen with me?" Luke's mother asked the stranger.

Apparently, she was a stranger to no one else. Luke returned to the family room and everyone else knew that her name is Diana, she moved in next door about six months ago, she is a nurse, and they even knew that she was coming over for Christmas. She had to work at the hospital later that afternoon, so she could not travel to spend Christmas with her family. She would be able to go in a few days, however, for a belated Christmas with her family. They were kind enough to wait until she could be there.

It was Diana who came out of the kitchen a short while later and announced to the family that Christmas dinner was ready. Everyone was ready. No one hesitated.

There was an unusually large number of people this year. Fortunately, the house was big enough to accommodate everyone. Between the dining room, breakfast room, and kitchen bar, there was exactly enough room for everyone. All three areas were in sight of each other, so no one felt left out. Luke's mother helped the four grandchildren with their seats at the kitchen bar. The adults could sit wherever they wanted – with three exceptions. Everyone knew that Luke's parents always sit at the two ends of the dining room table and Luke's mother made it clear that Luke was to sit next to Diana. That surprised no one. Even the young grandchildren probably knew why Diana was there.

After everyone was seated, Diana asked, "I feel so blessed to be here today. Do you mind if I am the one to say grace?"

In what was to become the first of two unforgettable Diana moments, she offered the most beautiful, heartfelt prayer that any of them had ever heard. More than one person used their napkin to dry their tears.

That solemn moment was soon replaced by lively conversation and laughter as they all enjoyed the absolute feast that Luke's mother had prepared.

It was certainly turning out to be the perfect Christmas, Luke thought to himself.

Not wanting to rush anyone, Luke's mother did remind them that Diana had to be at the hospital by three o'clock. They should all make their way to the family room for the gift exchange.

Luke's brother volunteered to play Santa Claus and hand out the packages. There were so many gifts that Luke offered to assist.

There were five large, identically wrapped, boxes off to one side. Luke reached for them first. He saw that they were from Diana. As he looked through the tags, he saw that there was one for his parents, one for his brother's family, one for his sister's family, one for his grandparents, and, surprisingly, one for him.

He walked over to his mother and whispered, "Why didn't you tell me that Diana was bringing gifts for everyone? I would have brought something for her."

"Oh, you did get her something. A diamond cross necklace," his mother whispered back, with a smile.

Luke was never one to create a scene, so he quickly returned to passing out the gifts without saying anything else.

With fourteen people unwrapping a mountain of gifts all at the same time, it did not take long for the room to be filled with torn wrapping paper, ribbons, and bows. Luke's sister went to the kitchen and came back with two large trash bags. Even though the unwrapping was still going on, she began to clean up the room a little.

It was not planned, and no one suggested it, but it seemed that all five of Diana's gifts were being opened at the same time. She had worked so hard on these gifts. She really hoped that everyone liked them. She stopped what she was doing and watched as each box was opened.

The talking and laughing stopped for a moment. The only sound in the room was the soft Christmas carols still playing in the background. Each family had received an exquisitely detailed painting of their house. The canvases were fairly large, eighteen by twenty-four, and elegantly surrounded by a gold leaf frame. And yes, Diana had painted them herself. Even Luke's mother had not been aware that Diana is an artist.

With her amazing pies at lunch and now her incredibly beautiful paintings, Diana had unintentionally, but certainly, overwhelmed Luke's entire family.

Diana had opened all but one of her gifts. The last one was a small box with a bow that was bigger than the box. The tag said it was from Luke. Diana certainly was not expecting a gift from Luke. He did not know her, and he did not even know she would be there. Unaware that all eyes seemed to be on her, Diana carefully opened the box and saw the lovely gold and diamond cross necklace. Tears immediately fell down her cheeks.

"Luke, why don't you put it on here," his mother happily suggested.

Luke carefully removed the necklace from the box and attempted to fasten it on her neck. His hands were trembling slightly, he did not know why, and it took him a couple of attempts to fasten it. He made a joke about his fat fingers.

It would all be explained then, by Diana, that she and Luke's mother had gone to the mall together to do Christmas shopping. Although they did not go into the jewelry store, Diana saw the cross in the window and talked about how beautiful it was. She had no idea how much it costs, but it was not something that she would buy for herself. Luke's mother got a crazy idea and now you know how that story ended.

With a trash bag in hand, Luke's sister went around the room picking up the last of the discarded gift wrapping. The talking and laughter had resumed as everyone sat admiring not only their own gifts, but all the gifts that everyone had received. They were each aware of how very blessed they were.

"This has been absolutely the best Christmas. I can't thank you all enough, but I can't be late for work, so I need to go," Diana said, with a touch of sadness in her voice.

"Luke, why don't you walk her home and help her with her packages," his mother suggested.

"I was just about to offer," Luke replied.

Diana made her way around the room, giving everyone a hug and a thank you. Each one expressed their gratitude to her.

As they arrived at her front door, Luke and Diana simultaneously went in for a hug.

"I know that your mother actually gave me the necklace, but

thank you for going along with her scheme," Diana said.

"I may have been kept in the dark about it for a while, but it actually is from me," Luke replied. His mother did trick him into paying for it, after all.

"I do hope that you like it," Luke said.

"I love it. When I saw it in the store, I never imagined getting it. It's kind of a dream come true," Diana replied.

"I hope you have a relatively stress-free day at work, and I hope you have a safe and wonderful trip to see your family. I'm sorry that you weren't able to spend today with them," Luke said.

"I miss them today, but otherwise, this was the perfect Christmas," Diana replied.

"Funny, that's what I was hoping for – a perfect Christmas," Luke said.

With that, Luke turned to walk back to his parents' house and Diana went into her own house to get ready for work.

Luke was gone for only a very few minutes, but he walked into a completely different setting. His grandparents had gone for a walk. His mother, sister, and sister-in-law were cleaning up the lunch mess. His brother had gone outside to get more firewood, and his brother-in-law was sitting on the floor with the children playing with their new toys. His father was napping in his recliner.

Luke just stood there and watched for a moment. It was a

perfect Christmas, he thought. He was so happy.

Later that evening, things began to return to normal. Everyone had helped themselves to leftovers, but that had now been put away. Everyone had left with all their Christmas goodies. The family room looked empty now, but in a good way.

The Christmas tree lights were still on, and the fireplace was still aglow, but no more wood was going to be used tonight. Luke and his parents were enjoying their conversation and their time together on his last night. Tomorrow he would have to return home. His mother usually persuaded him to stay until after lunch, but he thought he might get an earlier start. He really preferred getting home before dark.

"I know you made it for me to take home, but I think I'll have a little banana pudding. Would anyone else like something?" Luke asked.

"If there's any pecan pie left, I'll take a piece," his father replied.

"I'll put on a pot of coffee. Would you like a cup, dear?" his mother asked his father. She knows that Luke does not drink coffee.

"That sounds good," he replied.

Luke and his mother headed toward the kitchen, leaving his father still sitting comfortably in his recliner.

"What did you think of Diana? She's nice, isn't she?" his mother asked when they were alone in the kitchen.

"She's lovely. You have a good neighbor, I think. Did she buy the house or is she just renting?" Luke replied.

"Oh, she's buying. She says this is going to be her home for a long time. She really likes it here. She wants to settle down and have a family," his mother said.

Luke had already figured out his mother's motives and now saw where this conversation was going.

Bless his heart, he had no idea how this conversation would end, though.

"Do you think she might get you to come visit more often?" she asked.

"Family is my reason to come home, but I'll visit more often. I'll make that my New Year's resolution," Luke promised.

"You should give Diana a chance. I think you two would be a good match," she encouraged.

"I'm not really looking right now," Luke replied, hoping to end this conversation.

"Does that mean you have someone? What is her name? Why haven't you told us? You should have brought her with you for Christmas," she said, quite enthusiastically.

"Calm down. There's no one special in my life right now," Luke confessed.

"Well, don't you want to get married again?" she asked.

"I'm just not sure it's meant to be. If it happens, it happens," Luke replied.

"You can't just sit back and wait for it to happen. You have to make the first move and I think Diana would be your best match," she persisted.

"You need to forget Diana. I'm sorry, but that's just not going to happen," Luke insisted.

"You're not going to find anyone better than Diana. You must not want to get married again – or you would at least give her a chance," his mother said loudly, sounding a little exasperated.

"Why don't you want to get married again?" she asked, still loudly.

"I just don't think it's meant to be," Luke said as he picked up the desserts and walked toward the family room.

His mother followed him, carrying the coffee.

"What are you two yelling about?" his father asked as he took the piece of pecan pie from Luke.

"Luke said he's never getting married again," she replied as she handed him a cup of coffee.

"Why do you say that?" he asked.

"I didn't say never. I just said I don't think it's meant to be," Luke replied.

"Why would you think that?" his father asked, his voice getting a little louder than was necessary.

"I just don't think it's going to happen," Luke answered, really hoping that this conversation would come to a quick end.

"But why? Why do you say that?" his father asked in an extremely loud voice.

Luke suddenly heard his father's voice. Not his current voice, but his voice from the past. He heard him say, at his first wedding, that he would never attend another wedding – if Luke ever decided to do that again. He heard far too many horrible comments over the years that his father had made about "queers," the worst thing a person can be according to his father.

It was getting late, and Luke knew that if he told the truth about getting married again, his father would tell him to leave – immediately. Luke really did not want to start a six-and-a-half-hour drive at this hour.

Luke just sat there quietly, never answering his father's last question. Luke's father got up and left the room. They did not see each other for the remainder of the evening.

A few minutes later, his mother got up and went to the kitchen. There was nothing really to do in there, but she just piddled around for a while. Luke sat alone in the family room for a short while, just staring into the fireplace. Eventually, he got up and went to bed.

Well, at least most of day three was perfect. It is a shame it could not have ended that way, also.

December twenty-sixth is often a melancholy day. The excitement of Christmas is over, and it is just another routine day. It was a melancholy day for Luke, too, but not because the holiday was now over.

Luke woke up a little earlier than usual, but he did go to bed earlier than usual, as well. Normally, he would first go out and greet his parents. Today, he decided to shower, dress, and pack before doing anything else. He thought it would be best to get on the road as early as possible. His mother usually persuades him to stay until after lunch, but this time he was ready to go home.

Luke walked into the kitchen. His parents were sitting at the breakfast table, enjoying their morning coffee. They had both eaten and the plates were still on the table. The morning newspaper, obviously already read, was folded up and lying on the table as well.

Luke walked around to both parents, kissed them each on the cheek, and wished them a good morning.

Luke's father did not say anything. His mother asked what he wanted for breakfast.

"I'm not really all that hungry right now. I think I'll skip breakfast today," Luke replied.

There was no response from his mother.

Luke sat down at the table with them. After several minutes without a single word spoken, he got up and returned to his bedroom. He got his luggage and

Christmas gifts and took them to his car.

He walked past his parents and into the kitchen. He took a cola out of the refrigerator and walked back to the breakfast table.

"I think I'm going to head out now. It will be nice to get home before dark," Luke said.

There was no response from his father, but his mother stood up and followed him to the front door and stopped. Luke walked on to his car and opened the door. He waved goodbye to his mother and got in the car. He looked back at his mother. The front door was closed. She was gone.

Luke did not remember a single time before that both parents had not walked him to his car. There were always big hugs all around and they would both stand in the driveway continuing to wave until his car was out of sight.

Why couldn't today have been like that?

Chapter Two
New Year's Eve

It was a first for Luke – a black tie New Year's Eve party. Come to think of it, this was his first New Year's Eve party of any kind.

During his married days, he tried, on many occasions, to persuade Molly to go out for New Year's Eve, but she was never interested. She would not even stay awake until midnight. Luke would always quietly walk into the bedroom shortly after twelve, kiss her on the cheek, and say "Happy New Year, honey." He never got a response back.

Luke was excited about this party. There would be a silent auction (it is all for charity), dinner, dancing, and a champagne toast at midnight. Luke is not a drinker, but he was curious to taste champagne for the first time.

This party, an annual event, is also famous for its top-secret special guest, usually an A-list singer or other type of entertainer.

Being a dateless single man, Luke hoped to arrive at the party unnoticed. To hopefully achieve this, he decided to arrive a few minutes late, after everyone else was already inside. It did not exactly work out for him. The only parking was with a valet, and they seemed to be a little backed up.

Luke is not a huge fan of valet parking, but he had no choice at this event. A year or so ago, Luke attended a company function at a restaurant that offered valet parking. When he was ready to leave, the valet brought the car to the entrance and a woman with two small children immediately jumped it. When Luke calmly asked her to get out of his car, she did without saying a word. It took a little bit longer to get her two rambunctious children out of the back seat.

As Luke drove off, he looked at his rear-view mirror to see what she was going to do. He watched as she and the children got into a dark four-door car and drove away. Luke drove a light colored two-door car. He was convinced that she had just stolen someone's car.

Getting through the valet was not as time consuming has Luke thought it would be. Everyone was working quite efficiently.

The not for profit organization benefitting from tonight's event is the local zoo. It changes every year. It seems only fitting, then, that the theme for this year's party is animals. This was obvious before Luke even went inside.

A long, unusually wide sidewalk ran from the valet station to the front door. On the left side of the walkway was a life-size white elephant completely covered with crystals. Its trunk was uplifted and holding a giant crystal chandelier. A little farther down on the right side of the walkway was a life-size giraffe. It was also white and covered with crystals and held an identical crystal chandelier in its mouth. They made for a spectacular entrance.

At the front door, Luke waited in a short line as the partygoers presented their tickets.

Luke pulled out his wallet and took out his ticket. As he pulled the ticket out, another small piece of paper fell to the sidewalk. He bent down to pick it up. It was the card that the handsome stranger at the rest stop had given him. He had never looked at it and, in fact, had forgotten all about it. It was not a business card as Luke had thought. It was simply a social card with his name and contact information. He placed the card back in his wallet, just in case.

A momentary feeling of sadness washed over Luke. Here he was, looking quite handsome in a new tuxedo he bought especially for the occasion, attending the biggest party of the year, and he was all alone. Sure, he would know at least nine people at the party, the only reason he was invited is because he is single, but it still felt a little pathetic.

As Luke handed his ticket to the young lady at the door, she said, "Just one?"

"Yes. Pathetic, isn't it? Luke replied.

"Not pathetic at all. Just unusual. You are the only single ticket I have taken tonight. I apologize for even asking," the young lady said, wishing she could go back in time a few minutes and start all over.

This did not make Luke feel any better about his situation, but he was determined to enjoy the party and have a wonderful time.

Wanting nothing more than to see some familiar faces, Luke walked directly to his table.

Already sitting there were his boss, his wife and daughter, three of his co-workers, and their spouses. Luke took the empty seat next to the boss's daughter, sixteen-year-old Lily.

The sadness that Luke felt as he walked into the building dissipated like a morning fog over the lake. He was not aware that it was leaving until he realized that he was happy and enjoying himself immensely. The joy he felt so far, however, was nothing compared to the joy that was yet to come.

Midnight was fast approaching, and Luke thought this was a suitable time to take a discreet "nature walk." He could easily make it back to the table before the first note of Auld Lang Syne.

This was a large ballroom, so there were numerous restrooms from which to choose. Without giving it too much thought, he just walked to the one nearest his table. It was so quiet when he walked in that he assumed no one else was in there. The first room he entered had only the sinks and mirrors. The second room, his destination, had a row of urinals on the back wall and a long, padded bench along the opposite wall.

Sitting on the bench was a nice-looking man, approximately Luke's age. Luke assumed he was also a guest at the party because he was dressed in a tuxedo.

Luke passed him with a quick "hello" as he walked toward the urinals. Halfway across the room, Luke stopped and turned around.

"Are you all right? Can I get you something?" Luke asked.

"I'm fine. Just passing time," the stranger replied.

"Speaking of time. It is almost midnight. Are you planning to ring in the New Year in the men's room?" Luke asked jokingly.

"Well, since you asked, that is exactly what I plan to do," he replied.

Luke forgot for a moment the reason he was there and walked back and sat down on the bench.

"May I ask why?" Luke inquired.

"Have you ever been to one of these little shindigs?" he asked Luke.

"No, this is my first year. It's been wonderful so far," Luke replied.

"I was here last year, my first time. For some women here, midnight was just an excuse to see how many men they could kiss. I think they could sense that I was single and that just made it even worse," he told Luke.

"Are you still single?" Luke asked, curiously.

"I'm here with my parents. My mother is on the foundation's board of directors, and she really wanted me to come with them," the stranger explained. "My name is Caleb. So, what's your story?"

"Hi, Caleb. My name is Luke. My boss reserves a table for ten every year. He may know your mother. He used to be on the

board. Anyway, it is usually he and his wife and four couples from the office. He asks different people each year. This year he promised his sixteen-year-old daughter that she could come. That left a single ticket. I'm the only single person in our office, so lucky me,"
Luke explained.

"So, your date is sixteen years old?" Caleb joked.

"Very funny. Not my date," Luke insisted.

"Have you danced with her?" Caleb asked.

"Yes," Luke answered, almost embarrassed.

"She's your date," Caleb teased.

"I don't think I'm her type – and I know she's not mine," Luke insisted.

"Really? So, what is your type?" Caleb asked playfully.

Luke was not sure how to answer that.

"I guess I would have to say it would be someone sort of like you," Luke finally answered.

Luke wanted a little break in the conversation, and he had come to the men's room for a purpose.

"Will you excuse me for a minute? I did come in here for a reason," Luke said as he stood up.

Caleb did not say anything, but he did keep his eyes on Luke as he walked away and even while he was taking care of business.

With all that behind him, Luke returned to the bench and sat down beside Caleb, this time a little closer. Their minds were racing, but no one said anything for a few moments.

"I suppose everyone has a type; right?" Caleb asked rhetorically.

"If I just had to choose, it would be someone like you, I suppose," Caleb said, without looking directly at Luke.

Again, their minds were racing, but no one was speaking.

"Ten!"

"Nine!"

"Eight!"

The countdown to midnight had begun in the ballroom.

"You'd better hurry if you're going to get out there in seven seconds," Caleb said.

"I'm good. This is exactly where I'm supposed to be," Luke replied confidently.

"Three!"

"Two!"

"One!"

"Happy New Year!"

Luke gently reached up, placed both hands on Caleb's face, and kissed him like he had not kissed anyone in an awfully long time.

They pulled apart, ever so slightly, before Caleb reached for Luke's face and pulled him back for another, even longer, kiss.

"Happy New Year," said Luke.

"It certainly is so far. Happy New Year, Luke," Caleb replied.

It is not clear whose hand moved first, but they both reached for the other one's hand.

"Are you out at work?" Caleb asked.

"I came out once and swore I would never do it again. I just live my life," Luke replied.

"Good answer. So, if I come up to your table in a little while and ask you to dance, you won't have a problem with it?" Caleb asked.

"That would be no problem at all," Luke replied, smiling.

A few of the guests chose to leave shortly after midnight, but for most people, the party continued. Luke and Caleb danced, in each other's arms, for as long as they could.

Luke and Caleb both thought, finally, a New Year with promise.

Chapter Three
The Invitations

It did not take all that long really for Luke and Caleb to know, and very much appreciate, what they had together. This was certainly not the first relationship for either man, and they knew that it was different this time. It felt meaningful. It felt important. It felt permanent.

It became obvious early on that living apart was not acceptable. They both owned their own homes, which could have delayed their living together. Luckily, Caleb had a co-worker who had been telling him for a year that if he ever wanted to sell his condominium, he would buy it. When Caleb offered it to him, he did not hesitate for a minute.

Caleb soon moved into Luke's house, which they even talked

about eventually selling. They would then buy, or possibly build, their dream house together.

It was bedtime. Caleb stepped out of the shower, dried himself off, and combed his hair. Luke had showered earlier, so Caleb thought he would find him already in bed. Caleb walked down the darkened hallway to the bedroom, only to find the bed still made and no sign that Luke had been there.

Caleb walked back down the hall toward the living area and saw a faint light coming from the kitchen. Luke was sitting at the kitchen bar working intently on his laptop computer.

Caleb quietly slipped behind him, placed in hands on Luke's bare shoulders, and kissed the top of his head. Caleb tenderly slid his hands from Luke's shoulders down his torso. Luke lifted Caleb's right hand and kissed it. Luke then reached behind Caleb with both hands and grabbed his bare bottom.

"You're wearing my favorite outfit," said Luke.

"Just for you, my dear," replied Caleb.

"I'm just finishing here. I'll be ready for bed in just a minute," Luke assured him.

"What are you working on?" asked Caleb.

"Wedding invitations. I found a local calligrapher who will do them for us," Luke replied.

"But we talked about not sending formal invitations. It didn't really seem necessary," Caleb said.

"Yes, we did, but I still need to send out just four – to my family. It is not enough to bother with a printer. That's why I was looking for a calligrapher who could do individual invitations."

"It's fine, but why do you need to send written invitations to just your family?" Caleb asked.

Caleb pulled out a barstool and sat next to Luke.

"When Molly and I got married, we also decided against sending invitations. We personally invited our families and close friends. A wedding announcement, with Molly's picture, was published in four different newspapers. We figured that would cover everyone who might be interested. About a month before the wedding, I went down to spend a weekend with my parents. By this time, all wedding plans had been finalized. There was really nothing left to do. I was sitting with my parents in their living room. I do not remember what we were talking about, but I do know it had nothing to do with the wedding. My dad suddenly just announced that he would not come to our wedding unless he received a formal invitation in the mail. Before I could say anything, Mother politely reminded him that we were not sending our invitations. He just reiterated that he would not be there without a written invitation. I just wanted to keep the peace, so I assured him that he would get one in the mail. I also sent them to my grandparents and to my brother and sister," Luke explained.

"So that's all it's going to take to get them to come to our wedding?" Caleb asked.

"I really have no idea. I have never wanted to tell this story to anyone before, but you deserve to know. Obviously, my entire family did show up for the wedding. Everything was going well. Then two minutes – literally two minutes – before the ceremony was to start, my dad walked up to me and said, "If you ever do this again, don't expect me to be there."

"Oh my god, what did you do? What did you say?" asked Caleb.

I was so shocked by his words and his timing that I did not know what to say. I just said "okay" and then we walked out to the sanctuary."

"Did he ever tell you why he said that?" Caleb wanted to know.

"He never said, and I never asked. So, you see why it's anyone's guess whether or not they will come."

Luke closed his laptop and pushed it away. Caleb reached for Luke's hand.

"So, these invitations won't have my name on them, will they?" asked Caleb.

"I'm afraid not. That has to stay a secret. It is the only way to even possibly get them here. How upset are you?" Luke explained.

"I am not upset. I understand why you had to do it. I would rather trick them into coming than not have them at the wedding," said Caleb.

"I wish my family were more like your family. Then we would not even have to worry about this," Luke said.

"We've never really talked much about your first marriage. Is that subject off limits?" Caleb asked.

"Not at all. I just figured if you ever had any questions, you would ask," Luke replied.

"Well, I do have one question to start. Why?" Caleb asked.

"Why what?" Luke asked, not sure of the question.

"Well, I have no doubt that you loved Molly, but didn't it occur to you that maybe marrying a woman was not the best idea?" said Caleb.

"Long before I knew anything about the birds and the bees, I felt inside that I was not like other people. I just felt different. Years later, when I found out what that difference was, it made me feel even more different. I did not think there was anyone else like me, at least not anyone I knew. So, I figured that if I never told anyone, then no one would ever know my secret."

"And how long did it take before you knew that was not true?" Caleb asked, a little sarcastically.

"Longer than I care to admit. As you know, I like to stay at the office for a while after everyone else has gone home. It is usually the most productive part of my day. The cleaning crew starts at five o'clock and that's how I met Linda."

Best friend Linda? The Linda I'm finally going to meet at our wedding?" Caleb asked, excitedly.

"That's her. When I met her, she was working for the cleaning company that had the contract for our building. The conversations never got too personal, but we talked every day. On the Friday evening before my Saturday wedding, I wished her a happy weekend and got ready to leave. She wished me a happy weekend and then said, "I'll see you Monday." I told her I was going to be gone for a week. "Vacation?" she asked. I said I was going on my honeymoon. I will never, as long as I live, forget the look on her face or what she said."

Caleb, already holding hands with Luke, squeezed his hand tenderly.

"I didn't think you were the marrying kind."

"The sadness in her voice still haunts me. It was at that moment that I knew that my secret was not really a secret. I wondered how many other people knew about me," Luke confessed.

"Let us take a little detour in this conversation. How did Linda, the office cleaner, become Linda, the Payroll Manager?" Caleb asked.

"She didn't know it, but before my honeymoon, I had been working to try to get her hired by the company. She is so smart, valedictorian of her high school class, but she had only worked at a fast-food restaurant in high school and this cleaning job since graduation. I just knew she could do better than cleaning offices for the rest of her life. And I am not saying anything about people who clean homes, offices, cars, buildings, or anything else. It is honorable work. But Linda needed someone to give her a little push. No one else would. No one in her family had ever even dreamed of going to college, so she didn't either."

"That was really nice of you. Damn it, now I love you a little bit more," Caleb joked. "So, what happened when you got back from your honeymoon?"

"She was gone. I waited around for her to come in at five, but she did not show up. A little later, a different woman came in and started cleaning. When I asked her about Linda, she just said that Linda was working at another building. I wanted to talk to her in person, so the next day, I drove over to her house on my lunch hour. We had a nice heart-to-heart, we said what we needed to say, and she came back to work in my building. She agreed to go on an interview for the payroll clerk job I wanted her to have – and she got the job," Luke continued.

"She worked her way up to manager?" Caleb asked.

"She really worked for it. This company does not hire anyone for a management position unless they have a college degree. So, she worked full time and went to college full time. Luckily, the company pays for college – if you maintain a certain grade point average, 3.6, I think. So, she got her entire college education paid for. After she got her degree, she was eventually promoted to Payroll Manager. I'm so proud of her and we're still the best of friends," Luke concluded his story.

"Getting back to your story about Molly - so you got married and it lasted twelve years. Right? Were you sexually attracted to her?" Caleb wanted to know.

"I was a twenty-one-year-old virgin. I was sexually attracted to almost everyone," Luke replied, half-jokingly.

That answer left Caleb almost speechless, but he had so many more questions at this point.

"You were both virgins on your wedding night? I hope the wait was worth it," Caleb said, in almost disbelief.

"Well, I was a virgin in every way. I cannot really speak for Molly. We never talked about it. And our first time was not on our wedding night and, no, it was not worth the wait. If our first time had happened while we were dating, there probably never would have been a second time," Luke explained.

"But it got better?" Caleb asked.

"Yes, it got better," Luke admitted.

"You and I have made love many times. What did you think after our first time?" Caleb asked.

"Truthfully? I remember exactly what I was thinking. I almost said it aloud, but I stopped myself at the last second," Luke said.

"Why didn't you just say it?" Caleb asked, thinking he would have liked hearing it.

"I didn't want to scare you away. My thought was that I wanted to do that, with you, every day for the rest of my life," Luke admitted.

"Those were my thoughts, too. Really," Caleb confessed.

"OK, let us get back to you and Molly. When did you make love for the first time?" Caleb wanted to know.

"The Monday morning after the wedding," Luke replied.

"So, nothing on your wedding night and nothing the entire next day?"

"Nothing at all until Monday morning. I had to talk her into it then."

"I think it would be safe to say that she was a virgin when you got married," Caleb said, confidently.

"I certainly don't think she had ever had intercourse before, but I think she may have done other things – just not with me," Luke said.

"Why do you think that?"

"While we were dating, she casually mentioned her high school French teacher a couple of times. I do not remember what she said about him, but I do remember thinking that he was gay, and I wondered if she knew that. A few days after our wedding, she started talking about him a lot – almost every day. Most of us had our favorite teachers along the way, but it did not take me long to think that there was something not right about their situation. I was convinced, from her stories, that he is gay, so I never thought they had intercourse, but I was - I am - totally convinced that oral sex played a part in their relationship. After a while, she suddenly stopped talking about him and I haven't heard his name since."

"The night we met, you said that you came out once and would never do it again. Was that to Molly?" Caleb asked.

"About three months after we got married, I told her I was bisexual. I really wish I hadn't, but at the time it felt like a poison inside me that needed to come out."

"Were you afraid of what her reaction would be?"

"Not really. I honestly did not care what her reaction would be. I knew I would be fine either way."

"What was her reaction?"

"She said that it was part of who I am, that she loved all of me, and that she would love that part, too."

"That was a very mature response," Caleb said.

"I thought so. We never really talked about it after that night. It never was a problem – until it was."

"Did you fall in love with a man?" Caleb asked, not really believing that Luke would ever be unfaithful.

"Not at all. I did not change at all. She did. Out of the blue one night, she falsely accused me of having affairs with multiple men. She was yelling and screaming, and I was just wondering what the hell was happening. The whole conversation is a blur, but I do remember the last thing she screamed at me, "You can fuck the shit out of anyone you want to!" That was the moment our marriage ended," Luke said wistfully.

"Is that when you got divorced?" Caleb asked, thinking he already knew the answer.

"Oddly, no. We continued to live together, but sleep separately, for another eighteen months. Then she moved out," Luke explained.

"Have you invited Molly to our wedding?" Caleb asked.

"No. I never even thought about it. Should I? I wasn't invited to either one of hers," Luke replied.

"Either one? I didn't know she had ever remarried," said Caleb, actually quite shocked.

"She's been married and divorced twice since me," Luke said.

"You should invite her. We need to show her how it's done, set a good example," Caleb replied.

"If you're really OK with it, I'll invite her," Luke promised.

"Let us get back to your story. I still have some questions. You said that she falsely accused you. So, when did you have your first gay experience?"

"I've never told this before, but I like this story. It is right out of a romance novel. The very day that Molly moved out, a salesman named Kirby showed up at my office. I was not expecting him, and I have no idea how he got my name, but there he was. We chatted for a while, went over his product line, he left a catalog, and said he would follow-up later. I did not hear from him for about two and a half months. Suddenly, there he was again. No appointment. He just showed up one morning. I was interested in ordering from him, so I was happy that he came back. Maybe he had been waiting for me to call. Anyway, I placed an order and then walked him to the elevators. Before the elevator doors could open, he asked me out. I certainly was not expecting that, but I didn't hesitate to say yes," Luke went on.

"So, he was your first boyfriend?"

"Oh, no. We did go out twice, but on our second date, he told me that he was moving back to his hometown in Tennessee. He had already accepted a job there. I never heard from him again."

"That's a very sweet story, but a little sad," said Caleb.

"He was a lovely man. I'm glad that he came into my life when he did."

"I'm glad that he converted you."

"It didn't take much for me to see the light - and the error of my ways."

"You said you wanted to do it every day for the rest of your life. We haven't done anything today," Caleb reminded Luke.

"The day's not over," Luke said, with a kiss.

Chapter Four
The Wedding

If we think back to the New Year's Eve party six months ago, everyone there who saw Luke and Caleb together – and that was almost everyone at the party – could have predicted the future. That even includes Luke and Caleb. Even though they never said it aloud to anyone, they both thought the same thing by the end of the evening – I am going to marry that man.

It was just the natural progression of things. No one got down on one knee. No one proposed. No engagement rings were exchanged. By the time the subject of marriage came up, it was more about the details, like when and where. Whether or not the two of them were going to get married was never questioned.

When the subject of marriage was first brought up, that conversation was intertwined with talk of buying a new house together. They were both big projects, but for Luke and Caleb, they went hand in hand.

Some people search for months to find the "perfect" house, if there even were such a thing. Luke and Caleb were a little luckier than that. Their dream house did already exist – and they found it within one week.

They had tentatively set a date for their wedding. The question on their minds was if they could close on the new house and move in before that date. That seemed important because they immediately knew that their new back yard would be the perfect location for their wedding. They had talked of having the wedding and reception at the ballroom, where they first met, but this new idea seemed so much better.

The stars seemed to be aligned in their favor. Everything they wanted to do was possible. The wedding and reception would be at their new house. Their furniture and other stuff would be moved in, but they liked the idea of making their wedding night their first night in the new house. They had to stay someplace that night. Their flight to Hawaii for a honeymoon was scheduled for the following day. Everything was working out perfectly.

The big day finally arrived. If one could wish for, and receive, perfect weather for an outdoor wedding, it would look precisely like the lovely weather at the new home of Luke and Caleb. The sky was crystal blue with only a few white clouds casually floating overhead. The temperature remained in the low seventies all day, a rarity for June. Only the gentlest of breezes blew.

Admittedly, Luke and Caleb are both perfectionists. They both thought that if something as uncontrollable as the weather could be perfect, surely their carefully made plans would be as well.

Although Luke and Caleb had done the planning, they recruited a few of their best friends to help them bring the plans to life. These same friends also provided much needed assistance on the big day.

The first time Luke and Caleb saw this back yard, they knew that it would be a wonderful location for a wedding. The patio, which made up a large part of the back yard, would easily hold twice the number of guests they knew would be there. Beyond the patio was a pool and beyond that was a beautiful pool house. It was decided that the two grooms would get dressed in, and make their entrance from, the pool house.

Directly across the street from the house is a church. This has proved to be advantageous right from the start. Luke and Caleb attended services on the first Sunday after they looked at the house. They were both impressed in every way, but especially with Rev. Teena. She is a brilliant speaker. They have found their new church home.

Rev. Teena did not hesitate to say yes when Luke and Caleb asked her to perform the ceremony. She also offered the church parking lot for the wedding guests. That was a big relief because Luke and Caleb were not looking forward to having everyone searching for on-street parking. They even thought it may be necessary to hire a valet service – and you know how Luke feels about that.

A large purple and yellow banner was hung at the parking lot indicating that it was to be used by the wedding guests. In case that was not enough, their good friend Larry was stationed outside to greet guests and direct them to the parking lot and then to the back yard. To attract attention to the house, a large bouquet of purple and yellow flowers sat on a table on the sidewalk. Just to be sure that people knew what house to go to, large helium filled purple and yellow balloons were tied to the table. On the table were purple and yellow leis to give each guest. This was not a Hawaiian themed wedding, even though they were going to Hawaii for the honeymoon, but the leis were something that would connect everyone there. As you may have guessed, the official colors for the wedding are purple (heliotrope, to be exact) and buttercup yellow. Luke's favorite color has changed from time to time, but soft yellow has been his favorite for quite a while now. When Caleb was in high school, he ordered a shirt from Sears. It had French cuffs and the color was heliotrope. He had never heard that word before. As soon as he opened the box from Sears, that became his favorite shirt and heliotrope became his favorite color. The shirt is long gone, but his love of heliotrope remains. Luke and Caleb's attention to detail extended to the leis. The fabric leis were made of yellow flowers on one side and purple flowers on the other. In the center was a single purple and yellow flower. This color scheme would be used everywhere.

The catering service was the first to arrive, followed by the six friends who were helping. Last, but not least, to arrive were the photographer, his assistant videographer, and Rev. Teena. Everyone knew exactly what to do when the guests started arriving.

To assist in making this a drama-free afternoon, Larry familiarized himself with photographs of both Luke's and Caleb's families. Luke's family was to be escorted to the living room and Caleb's family to the family room. They would be escorted to the back yard just moments before the wedding were to begin. Luke really did not want the two families to meet, and talk, before the wedding.

Everyone was seated, friends and family, and the show was about to begin.

Mary sat down at the organ, which had been moved from inside. Tom stood beside the organ and began to sing. The guests, who had been in, shall we say, active conversation began to settle down. After Tom sat down, the music continued and the doors to the pool house opened. Two small wooden bridges, painted white, had been built across the pool. One was covered in yellow flowers, the other in purple. Luke and Caleb came out of the pool house, and each walked across their personal bridge.

Luke's family were quite confused about who Caleb was. Most of them assumed that he was Luke's best man.

When the two of them reached their destination, and then were joined by Rev. Teena, it became clear to everyone who Caleb was.

Luke's father began to stand. He did not get far up before his mother placed her hand on his leg and forced him to remain seated. She did not say anything, but she spoke volumes with her eyes.

The wedding continued without interruption until Rev. Teena made the standard command, "You may kiss your husband."

Just as Luke and Caleb embraced and kissed for the first time as husband and husband, Luke's father stood and, with his hands, indicated to his family to stand. They were leaving.

The other guests at the wedding, who were already cheering and applauding as Luke and Caleb kissed, read something entirely different into Luke's father's actions. Everyone stood up, cheering, and applauding even more enthusiastically. As Luke's family began their walk down the center aisle, four confetti cannons blasted purple and yellow glittery confetti over the crowd.

Luke and Caleb were unaware of any confetti cannons, so the shock of it interrupted their kiss.

"Don't worry. We'll clean it up," someone shouted, and the kiss resumed.

The confetti explosion did one of two things. Either it took the focus away from Luke's family leaving – or it brought it to everyone's attention because they were all looking around at the confetti as it fell.

Luke, although quite occupied, did notice his family

leaving. However he felt about it, he kept his feelings to himself.

Although he did not really expect anyone to leave before the reception, Larry was prepared, just in case. The table that had once held leis now held gift bags for all the guests to take with them. As Luke's entire family rushed by, Larry offered them their bags. When everyone declined, Larry insisted. He was able to convince each of them, except for Luke's father, to take a bag. If Larry had been aware of their behavior in the back yard, he may not have been quite so insistent.

Without exception, everyone else at the wedding made their way into the house for the reception. Even if there had been some doubt before, everyone now knew exactly what had happened outside. Everyone was worried about Luke and how he must be feeling. Some people were wondering if they should leave. One brave soul asked Luke if he would like for everyone to leave. They genuinely wanted to be sensitive to Luke's – and Caleb's – feelings.

The dining table looked like it was set for a Palm Court– style afternoon tea, with the addition of the white, purple, and yellow masterpiece, the massive wedding cake. Luke and Caleb, with their arms lovingly wrapped around each other, stood at the end of the table, next to the wedding cake. Although there were many people in the house, most of them could see the newlyweds. The others, at least, could hear everything.

Luke wanted to address the issue of what had happened in the back yard.

"Before we go on with the party, Caleb and I would like to thank each one of you, sincerely, for being here today. It is such a wonderful feeling to be surrounded by the people we love – and who love us in return," he began.

"Contrary to what you may think, nothing bad, or even unexpected, happened today. We are extremely happy that my family was here to share in our wedding. It will, without a doubt, take a little while before they share in our marriage. One of them will take longer than the others. But that is all right. The important thing is that there are no more secrets. There never should have been, but I cannot go back in time and change anything," he continued.

"Now, I do not know about you, but I haven't had a thing to eat all day. I want a big piece of this cake – and one of everything else on this table," he concluded.

And the joy continued.

Chapter Five
Conclusion

It was now September, exactly three months since the wedding. If you were to ask either Luke or Caleb about the past three months, they would both say that it was the best three months of their lives. The marriage was going very well.

On their first month anniversary, they celebrated at a restaurant that they had both wanted to try for a while. They enjoyed it so much that they decided to go there for all their monthly anniversaries, but not on other dates. They wanted to keep it special. Both men were very much looking forward to this evening, but they had to first get through their workdays.

It used to be quite common for Luke to stay at work longer

than his colleagues. He enjoyed the solitude and he always said that he got more work done when no one else was around. Of course, that all changed when Caleb came along. He now has a reason to go home.

On this particular day, when it really mattered that he leave work on time, his boss informed him, quite reluctantly, that he would be needed in the office that evening. His boss had been at the wedding, and he knew what this day meant to Luke, but he assured Luke that there was no other way. He promised Luke, and everyone else, that he would let them go as early as possible.

It was a telephone call that he really did not want to make, but Luke had to call Caleb to let him know of the change of plans. The conversation went much better than Luke had expected.

"That's fine. You do what you must do. I'll call and cancel our reservation and I'll have dinner ready for you when you get home," Caleb replied. "Is there anything in particular that you would like?"

"No, not that I can think of. Anything you fix will be delicious," Luke answered.

With that, both men returned to their work, still very much looking forward to the evening together.

Caleb heard the garage door opening. He did not wait for Luke to come in. He went out to the garage and greeted Luke – with a kiss or two, of course. Both men were so happy to see each other.

As they walked into the house, Luke could not help but comment, "Something certainly smells good. What did you make?"

"It's a surprise, but I think you will be happy. I will say, though, that I made a Banana Pudding for dessert," Caleb replied.

"My mother's recipe?" Luke asked.

"Of course. There's no better," Luke assured him, smiling.

"Why don't you go change out of that suit while I get everything on the table?" Caleb suggested.

Another kiss and Luke was off to the bedroom to change.

Luke returned to the kitchen, where Caleb was, and they walked together to the dining room. At first, Luke just stood there and stared at the table. For the first time, Caleb had pulled out "the good stuff" to set the table. This was a special occasion, after all. Then Luke noticed the food.

"Is all of that from Alexander's?" Luke asked.

"When I called to cancel our reservation, Alexander himself answered the phone. He seemed more upset about the cancelation than I was. He just insisted "if you can't come to Alexander's, Alexander's will come to you.""

"All of this food was delivered just a few minutes before you got home," Caleb replied. "I'm surprised you didn't see the delivery truck."

"Alexander wasn't even going to take any money for all of this, but I absolutely insisted. He sort of got his way, though. The delivery man handed me a gift certificate for us 'to use next month.”

"Speaking of deliveries, what is this box on the dining table?” Luke asked.

"It came today. It's addressed to both of us, but I thought you should be the one to open it,” Caleb replied.

"Why is that?” Luke asked.

"Look at the return address,” Caleb suggested.

The package was from Diana, the wife who could have been. Luke went to the kitchen to get a box cutter and came back and opened the large box. He pulled out a package gift wrapped in purple and yellow – and a letter. Luke handed the package to Caleb.

"You open the gift while I read the letter," Luke said.

Caleb took the package and Luke opened the letter and began reading it aloud.

"Dear Luke and Caleb: I hope this finds you both well and happy," the letter began.

"I was visiting your mother when your wedding album was delivered. First, let me say how impressed we both are. I have never known anyone to send their relatives leather-bound albums of their wedding pictures. Most people just put loose photos in an envelope. This is lovely. I was still there when your father got home from work. Your mother immediately told him about the album. He refused to look at it and he told your mother to destroy it. I am so sorry to tell you all of this. Obviously, your mother did not want to destroy it, so I told her that I would take care of it," Luke continued reading, then wiping tears from his eyes.

By now, Caleb had carefully unwrapped the gift that Diana sent. Based on the shape of the gift, they had both figured out what it was even before Caleb unwrapped it. It was a gorgeous painting of their new home. Caleb held it up so that Luke could see it. Luke took it from Caleb and just stared at it for a moment.

"This is amazing. We'll hang it next to her other painting," Luke said.

He returned the painting to Caleb and continued reading the letter.

"By taking care of it, I simply meant that I would take it home with me. There is absolutely no way that I would ever destroy it. I will hold on to it as long as necessary, but if you want me to, I will send it back to you. (But I really want to keep it.) Luke, I know that you have not spoken to your parents since the wedding."

"You haven't?" Caleb interrupted.

Luke continued reading, "I'm not trying to speak for anyone else, but I honestly believe that most people in your family really want to see you and they want to meet Caleb and get to know him. I hope you will plan a trip soon to visit with everyone. I have a lovely guest room that, so far, has never been slept in. You are both welcome to stay with me if that would make things easier for you."

Luke looked up at Caleb and Caleb simply shook his head up and down.

"I hope you enjoy the painting, but please do not feel any obligation to display it. Everyone seemed to appreciate the paintings last Christmas, so I thought you would enjoy one of your new house. I promise, though, no more paintings. (smiley face emoji) With much love and best wishes, Diana," Luke concluded.

Luke put the letter down on the table and looked at Caleb.

"What do you think about Diana's offer?" Caleb asked.

"More importantly, how do you feel about it?" Luke asked.

"I very much want to take her up on it. Your family is going to be my family for the rest of our lives. I really want to get to know them – and I want them to know me," Caleb assured Luke.

And that called for a very enthusiastic kiss.

"I love you," they said, in unison.

The Love Continues